CLAIMING THE RUNAWAY

EMMA BRAY

CHAPTER ONE

Hadley

MY WHOLE BODY tenses up as I hear the soft opening of my bedroom door. I peek over my covers to see Randal's form outlined in the darkness. My heart speeds up as he stumbles over to my bed, and I sit up, scooting back against the headboard.

"What are you doing in here, Randal?" I whisper frantically, panic gripping my chest. He's drunk—again. My stepdad is a real piece of shit. He's always been a sleazeball, but he's been getting drunk more often lately.

I've been afraid something like this might happen.

He's been finding little ways to touch me more and more lately. A hand on my hip as he reaches around me in the kitchen to grab the cereal box out of the cabinet. A touch on the knee when we're watching TV. I always find a way to leave the room when he does that, his touch making me shiver with dread and disgust.

Of course, my mom doesn't notice. She doesn't know where she is half the time. She stays doped up on pills. That's all she cares about anymore. I think she might have loved me at some point. Maybe she still does in her own way, but she's never lucid enough to talk to me or tell her sleazy husband to keep his hands off her daughter.

"Hadley," he slurs my name as he sits down on the edge of my bed. "I came to see you, babygirl." My mind revolts at the way he calls me *babygirl*.

"I'm sleeping, and you need to leave," I try to reason with him.

"Aw, don't be like that, babygirl," he says leaning down over me, pinning me to the bed. I feel panic starting to rise within me when I feel a certain part of his anatomy pressing against my thigh. I almost retch when I realize what it is and that he's turned on.

I push against his chest, but he's so much bigger than me. Randal isn't a small man by any means. His beer belly alone is enough to pin me to the mattress, and I feel a scream bubbling up in my throat.

This is not happening. This is not happening. My drunk stepdad is not fixing to rape me.

I know I should have left two days ago when I turned eighteen, but I'm scared. I have no money, no job. I have nowhere to go. I figured I'd take my chances here until I find a job—that way I won't be sleeping on the streets.

I'm starting to think the streets might be a better option, though.

"Dammit," he curses, slapping a hand over my mouth as I scream and twist underneath him, desperately trying to throw him off me.

"Be quiet you little bitch," he hisses at me, pressing harder against me. "Don't act like you don't want this. Walking around this house in those tight little shorts of yours. Goddamn little cock tease."

He raises his hips for just a moment as he tries to undo his pants, and I take the opportunity. Acting on instinct, I bring my knee up and ram it into him—hard.

He gasps in pain, his hands going down to grasp between his thighs as I slip out from under him, running toward the door.

"Hadley!" he screams. "You get your ass back here!"

I don't know how long my kick will have him down, and I'm running off pure adrenaline, my only thought to get out of here as fast as I can, so I run out the front door and take off down the sidewalk, not taking the time to stop to put on shoes.

We live just a block from downtown. If I can make it to a business that's open, I can slip inside long enough to get my bearings and figure out what I'm going to do.

I hazard a glance back and see Randal coming out of the door to the house, looking pissed as hell. My mother is nowhere in sight. She probably didn't even wake up amidst all the commotion.

I redouble my efforts and turn to the left to get out of his line of sight, running into the first lit-up business I see, not even stopping to check what it is.

Damon

I lift my shot of whiskey to my lips, but before I ever take the drink, a commotion at the front of the bar draws my eyes.

I lay the untouched shot down and glance over at

the girl who's just burst through the door like the hounds of hell are nipping at her heels.

My eyes trail down her lithe frame. She's wearing butt-hugging shorts that don't leave much to the imagination the way they grip her juicy little ass and a form-fitting tank top that shows off a pair of perfectly pert little breasts. Hair as dark and thick as a raven's wing cascades around her shoulders. Her chest is heaving, and I notice that her feet are bare. I frown. She looks like a scared little rabbit.

From the hoots and whistles that come from a table of drunken fools near the front of the bar, I realize I'm not the only one who's noticed her haphazard entrance.

She ignores the catcalls and attempts to walk over to an empty table to sit down, but one of the pricks gets up and follows her.

"Hey, babe, you looking for some company?" he slurs. I can hear him all the way over here.

She shakes her head, clearly not interested.

He sits down in the booth next to her and slides close to her. She shrinks away from him, pressing herself against the wall, and I've seen about all I can take. If there's one thing I can't stand, it's drunken assholes forcing their attentions on unwilling women.

I down my shot in one gulp, slap the shot glass

back down on the counter, and walk over to where she's sitting.

"I think she's made it clear she's not interested, buddy," I tell the drunken idiot who insists on imposing himself on her.

"Hey, why don't you mind your own—" he begins, but then he stops mid-sentence and gulps when he looks up and sees who's talking to him.

Yeah, I guess my reputation precedes me.

I raise an eyebrow at him. "You want to finish that sentence?"

He quickly slides out of the booth, apologizing, "No, Damon, man, I didn't realize it was you."

I say nothing else to him, staring at him menacingly as he scampers away back to the table where his crew sits guffawing like the morons they are.

I look back down at the girl and am almost bowled over by the most innocent-looking, sapphire blue eyes I've ever seen. They're framed by thick, dark lashes, and my chest tightens painfully.

Jesus, I knew she was beautiful from the glimpse I got of her across the bar when she burst into the place, but up close, she's nothing short of a fucking angel.

Her skin is porcelain, the cheeks tinged pink from her exertion, and her lips are sinfully full and rosy, the kind of lips that give teenage boys wet dreams.

I feel myself beginning to stiffen in my jeans just looking at her face. Fuck, this girl is a princess, and I'd love nothing more than to spoil her for all she's worth.

I realize I'm staring at her, so I gather my wits long enough to ask her, "Do you mind if I sit?"

She shakes her head, "No." Then, she blushes, "I mean, no, I don't mind if you sit, that is." Fucking adorable. She's fucking adorable. Everything about her.

I sit in the booth across from her, smelling her scent from across the table. She smells young and sweet, like fresh berries just waiting to be plucked. I fight back a groan.

Fuck, what's wrong with me? No female has ever affected me this way.

"What's your name?" I ask her.

"Hadley," she answers.

"Hadley," I repeat, tasting her name on my tongue. "I'm Damon."

She nods, "So I heard from that guy. Thanks for helping me just now, by the way," she says, tucking a strand of that long, dark hair behind her ear. My fingers itch to reach out and see if those locks are as soft and silky as they look.

"No problem," I tell her. "Some guys are just idiots when they drink."

She looks down, "Yeah, tell me about it."

I frown, not liking the sadness in her tone. "What are you doing in a place like this?" I ask her.

She looks up, "Oh, um, I was just...taking a break from my walk."

I cock my head to look pointedly under the table at her bare feet. "You always take a walk barefoot in the middle of the night?" I ask her. There's more to her story than she's letting on, and I'm damn sure going to get to the bottom of it.

Her face colors even more. "I—I," she sputters before her shoulders sag and she finally admits "I was running away from something."

"Something or someone?" I ask, already reading between the lines, and what I'm sensing has my hands fisting on the table. If someone hurt her, I'll hunt them down and tear them limb from limb with my bare hands.

"My stepdad," she confesses, finally looking back up at me. "He's been drinking more lately, and he...he came into my room tonight."

Hot anger boils through me, but I attempt to tamp it down as I ask her, "Did he hurt you?"

She shakes her head vehemently. "No, I kneed him in the balls and took off before he could really do anything."

"Good girl," I immediately tell her.

She pales as her eyes meet something over my shoulder. I turn to look at the door where some drunk has just stumbled in. He's a big, pot-bellied mother-fucker, but I'm still taller and bigger than him—the difference being I'm all muscle. I did nothing but work out in prison, trying to make myself stronger and pass the time the only way that kept me sane.

"Is that him?" I ask as I turn back to her, only to see an empty booth staring back at me.

"Fuck," I swear under my breath as I see her heading for the back of the bar. I don't know where she thinks she's going, but she won't be getting out that way.

I chase after her and catch up with her just as she's fixing to enter the ladies' room.

"Hey, baby, hold up," I tell her, gently grasping her arm.

She turns to me, gasping, her eyes wide. She relaxes when she sees it's me, and that fills me with an undeniable sense of pride that she must feel somewhat safe with me.

"I have to get out of here," she says desperately.

While I want nothing more than to march back out there and beat her stepdad's ass, setting her mind at ease and not losing her is more important, so I nod before wrapping my arm around her waist and steering her toward the kitchen. "Come on. I know a way out the back."

I'm friends with the owner, so I come and go as I please, using whatever entrance I please, and no one bats an eyelash. I steer her through the kitchen and out the back door into the alley.

I lead her around the front to where my black SUV is parked and open the passenger door for her. "Get in," I nod at the SUV.

She hesitates for only a moment before she glances back at the bar where her stepdad is probably still inside looking for her before she obeys and slides into the seat.

I shut the door behind her before walking over to the driver's side.

I don't know what act of fate brought us together tonight, but I vow to myself now that fucker will never get near her again. No one will ever hurt this princess again if I have anything to say about it.

Hadley

I glance over at the man in the driver's seat. He's huge —bigger even than Randal, but somehow I sense that he won't hurt me.

His muscles bulge underneath the sleeves of his black short-sleeved shirt. He's wearing a silver chain around his neck along with a leather necklace too. The exposed parts of his arms are covered with ink. I wonder if his chest is tatted too.

His hair is dark and cropped close to his head. Stubble lines his jaw, casting shadows on his face.

He's wearing jeans, and I can see how huge and muscular his thighs are in them. His legs seem to take up the entire front of the SUV.

"Where are we going?" I ask him softly. It strikes me that I should be more worried than I am. I'm in the car with a stranger, letting him take me to some unknown destination, yet I don't feel a fraction of the fear I've felt every night living in the same house as my stepdad.

I just feel...relief. Relief to be putting some distance between me and my would-be assailant.

"My place," he answers gruffly. "I can't leave you out here alone with no shoes and nowhere to go."

"What makes you think I don't have anywhere to go?" I ask him.

He raises an eyebrow at me, his gray eyes flashing over to me knowingly. "Do you?"

I look away from him before admitting, "No."

When I look back over at him, he's frowning, and his hands seem to tighten on the steering wheel. "So, what were you planning on doing?"

I shrug. "Honestly, I don't know. I just acted on fight or flight instinct, you know? I just had to get as far away from him as I could. I figured I'd figure the rest out as I went along."

"How old are you?" he suddenly asks me.

"I turned eighteen a couple of days ago," I answer. "I should have left then, but I've been looking for a job so I could afford a place to stay when I left."

The hopelessness of my situation washes over me, and I feel a knot of anxiety form in my tummy.

"You can stay with me," he offers.

I look at him in surprise. "I couldn't possibly—"

He cuts me off with, "As long as you need to. I've got an extra bedroom."

I look up at him, trying to gauge whether he's serious or not or whether he's just being nice because he feels sorry for me, but what does it matter anyway?

I look down at my bare feet that I know are cracked and bleeding. I don't even have any shoes.

What choice do I really have?

Damon

"I was thinking about getting a roommate anyway," I add when she's silent. That's not true, but I could have thought of getting one. What is true is that I have a two-bedroom apartment. It was all that had been available at the time, and I'd needed somewhere to live immediately, so I took it. If it gets her to stay, that's all that matters. Suddenly, it's more important to me than ever that she stay with me where I can make sure she's safe.

"Maybe just for tonight," she concedes.

"As long as you need," I add firmly.

She doesn't say anything for a long moment, but when she finally does, she just says, "Thank you." Her tone is genuinely grateful, and it tugs at my heart. When is the last time anyone was truly grateful for anything I had to offer?

I pull into the parking lot and kill the engine before getting out of the car and going around to open her door.

She winces when she steps from the SUV and puts weight on her feet, so I reach down and scoop her into my arms without a word. This little bunny is injured, but I'm going to take care of her now.

Her arms go around my neck as she meekly protests, "I can walk."

"You're hurt," I tell her simply before settling her against my chest. Fuck, she feels so good pressed against me, and that sweet berry scent wafts up to me. I have to fight against inhaling deeply. I want to eat her up. I bet she tastes just as sweet as she fucking smells.

She weighs nothing, and I feel my cock starting to harden and press against the zipper of my jeans again as I think of how close my arm is to her barely legal pussy.

Shit, I haven't been with a women since I got released six months ago, but I know that's not what's fueling my desire for her. I'm not just hard up for a quick fuck. I could have gotten that a long time ago if that's all I want. I've refrained from being with anyone since I've gotten out because I've been busy rebuilding my life, making something of myself. Plus, I'm just into casual sex anymore. I have two capable hands to take care of my needs with and decided if I'm ever with a woman again, it will be because I want her—all of her.

It suddenly hits me like a ton of bricks. I've been waiting.

I've been waiting for *her*. For Hadley. This sweet little angel I have cradled in my arms right now.

Don't ask me how the fuck I know this. I just fucking do. Something deep inside me calls to me to protect her. To worship her.

Nothing has ever felt so right as holding her. My arms instinctively tighten around her as I carry her up the outdoor stairs to my apartment.

I set her gently down long enough to fish the key from my pocket, and then I hoist her back up into my arms to carry her across the threshold.

She doesn't protest at all. She just lays in my arms trustingly as I carry her over to lay her on the couch.

I look down at her with her dark hair fanning out all around her, her lips full and lush, her eyes wide, and I know in that moment I'm never going to be able to let her go.

CHAPTER TWO

Hadley

DAMON TENDS to the wounds on my feet before he shows me to my room. It's humbling to see this huge giant of a man kneeling before me and carefully handling my tiny feet like they're made of the most delicate glass. The way he cares for me, his huge yet gentle hands tenderly cleaning the blood from my feet before applying salve and wrapping them gives me a warm feeling inside. When was the last time anyone took care of me? Maybe my mom did at some point a long time ago, but if she had, it was when I was too young to remember. All I remember of my mom now is her glassy, half-there look as she stays in a pill-induced haze.

He gives me one of his T-shirts and a pair of sweatpants to wear, and then he shows me to my room and gives me my privacy, telling me he's just next door if I need anything. Again, that little ball of warmth settles in my stomach at someone caring for me. I don't know why he's doing it. Maybe he's just a nice guy underneath his hard-looking veneer, but I gratefully accept his kindness, realizing that if it hadn't been for him, I'd probably still be out on the streets.

I put the shirt on after I awkwardly take a quick shower, taking care not to mess up the wrappings on my feet. His shirt smells like him, and I take a deep breath, inhaling his scent of laundry detergent and something decidedly masculine and woodsy.

The shirt hangs down below my knees, and the sleeves come down below my elbows. That's how much bigger than me he is. I try the pants, but they fall off my hips even after I roll them up several times, so I finally just pull them back off. The shirt is long enough to cover me anyway. I'm not wearing a bra or panties, but I'm just going to be sleeping in here alone anyway, so it doesn't really matter.

I lay in the softest bed I think I've ever lain in,

enjoying the feel of the soft cotton sheets. I burrow deeper under the covers and curl onto my side.

Can I possibly take him up on his offer and stay here with him? I don't really know him, but somehow I instinctively know he'd never hurt me. If he was going to do that, he's had plenty of opportunity already, and he wouldn't have taken the time to bandage me up.

And something also tells me he's the kind of guy who doesn't say things he doesn't mean, so if he offered me a room, he must really mean it. He didn't have to offer me one, so why would he offer it unless he meant it?

My mind starts swirling toward how I have to get a job and basically start my life from scratch. There's no way I'm going to chance going back home to get any of my belongings—not that I have much to my name anyway. Just a few clothes, but I can get new clothes. It's not worth the risk of running into Randal again just to get some clothes. I wish I'd had the presence of mind to snatch some up or at least grab some shoes before I fled.

It doesn't take long for my thoughts to begin to die down, despite myself. The softness of the bed and the allure of sleep pull me under until I sleep long and deep—better than I ever have in my whole life—and finally, for once in my life, feeling completely safe.

Damon

I can't fucking sleep. Just knowing nothing but a wall separates me from Hadley's ripe young body is enough to keep my cock rock hard all night. I'm only twenty-six, but I'm a felon and have no right to be thinking of such an innocent angel the way I am.

The things I want to do to her...and right after she just ran away from home because of her perverted stepfather...they should lock my ass back up right now.

I look over at the weight set sitting in the corner of my master suite. That would be a great way for me to work off some of this extra adrenaline, but I'm afraid the clanging of the weights would wake up Hadley, and she needs to sleep.

My fists clench when I think of her scumbag stepfather trying to put his hands on her—of any man trying to put his hands on her. My fingers itch to beat him to a pulp, but I take a deep breath and remind myself that she's safe here with me now. Although I flattened my time so I'm not on papers, if I hunt the fucker down and commit murder, I'll get thrown back in the pen, and I won't be able to protect her if I'm locked up in there.

No, Hadley is my number one concern now. I've just been going through the motions for so long, existing. Now I have a reason to live. Even if she never wants me as anything more than a friend, I have to protect her. I have to be in her life, and I'll take whatever I can get—even if it's only a platonic relationship as her roommate.

I glare down at my cock. *Platonic, my ass*, it seems to scream at me. *We want her. Make her ours.*

My balls feel heavy just thinking about claiming her. I want to mark her as mine and snarl like a feral beast at any other man who even glances her way.

But I want her trust more. I don't ever want her to run away from me. I want her to feel comfortable enough with me to stay with me.

I slide the covers from my body and pull on a pair of sweatpants. It's obvious I'm getting no sleep tonight.

I walk to her bedroom door and silently turn the knob. I peek in to see her curled up on her side asleep, her dark hair fanning out around her. She looks so tiny with the covers pulled up to her chin, and desire hits me like a brick in the chest. I softly close the door back, satisfied that she's okay and sleeping soundly before I walk resolutely back to my bathroom and force myself to taking a freezing cold shower in hopes of making my stubborn dick go down.

I finally get it down enough to catch a couple of hours of sleep. When I wake up, Hadley still isn't up, so I go into the kitchen and start cooking breakfast. I don't know what she likes to eat, so I make an assortment of foods, hoping something will please her.

Just as I'm plating the pancakes up, I hear her door open, and a minute later, she's padding into the kitchen.

I damn near drop the plate when I see her wearing nothing but my shirt, her dark hair mussed and her eyes still sleepy. All she needs is lips swollen from my kisses and she'd have that incredibly sexy, just-fucked look down pat.

"Good morning," she says shyly.

"Good morning, Hadley," I answer her, my voice coming out more gravelly than I intend. I clear my throat. "What happened to the pants?"

"Oh," she looks down at her bare legs and blushes. "They were too big and kept sliding off, so I stopped fighting the battle."

Of course, I should have known she wouldn't be able to get them to stay up. She's just a little slip of a thing.

My gaze rakes over her again, noticing the little bumps of her nipples that let me know she's not wearing a bra. I wonder if she's wearing panties, and the thought that nothing is separating her naked body from me but my shirt has my cock instantly hardening.

I turn from her to try to hide my growing arousal. Fuck me. I can't be getting impossibly hard every time she walks into the room if she's going to stay with me.

But *fuck*...I can't help it. Her fucking *existence* is enough to torture my dick.

"I'll go get you some clothes today," I tell her before I motion for her to have a seat. "I didn't know what you liked, so I made a little bit of everything." The table is covered with bacon, eggs, toast, and pancakes.

She looks down at everything and smiles, her cheeks dimpling. I can't help but wonder if she has dimples in other places.

"This all looks amazing," she says, "but you didn't have to go to all this trouble for me."

"I gotta eat anyway," I point out. I sit a cup of coffee in front of her and watch as she adds cream and sugar to it.

I drink mine black and try not to stare at her as she forks a bite of pancakes, her lips sliding off the fork as she places the bite in her mouth, closing her eyes and moaning. *Jesus*, she even looks sexual when she eats. Everything about her screams sex.

A bit of syrup glistens from the corner of her

mouth. I want to lick it off as I taste her, but instead I just reach my hand up and brush it away with the pad of my thumb.

Her breath hitches when I touch her. The skin of her cheek is velvety soft. "You've got some syrup..." I explain, my voice gruff.

"Oh," her voice is breathy when she speaks, "thanks."

I contemplate leaning in to kiss her. I don't think she'd push me away if I did right now, but it's probably too soon after what she just went through, so I pull back instead and spear a spoonful of my eggs, shoveling them into my mouth.

After I swallow, I take a swig of my coffee before telling her, "I'll stop by the store after work and pick you up some things. You can just hang out here today until I get you some clothes."

Her face colors. "You really don't have to do that. You've already done so much."

My lips tip up, "As much as I don't mind you wearing nothing but my shirt all the time, I think you'll need more substantial clothing if you ever want to go out again."

She blushes, and it's the prettiest thing I've ever seen. My little rabbit.

She sits up straighter in her chair as she says, "I'll pay you back every cent once I get a job."

"Okay," I say simply, sensing that she needs this to feel like she's maintaining her dignity, although I couldn't care less if she ever pays me back.

She nods as if it's all settled and relaxes again, and I can't help but respect her sense of pride. It's the same type of pride I have, intent on working for myself and not depending on anyone else, though I wouldn't mind her depending on me for everything.

"Did you mean it?" she suddenly asks.

My brows furrow. "Mean what?"

She fidgets in her chair, looking like a timid little schoolgirl as she tucks her hair behind her ear. "Were you serious when you offered me a room here?"

"Of course I was, sweetheart," the endearment just slips out, and I don't regret it. It feels natural to call her that because that's what she is. She's a total sweetheart, *my* sweetheart, whether she knows it or not. "As long as you want to."

She smiles up at me shyly again as she says, "Thank you, really. I don't know what I would have done if I hadn't run into you. And I'll pay you back everything. I swear."

"It's nothing," I assure her, although it's *everything*. *She's* everything.

Hadley

I insist on doing the dishes when Damon stands and begins loading them into the sink.

"No, really. It's the least I can do," I tell him. I want to feel useful. I *need* to feel useful.

His gray eyes appraise me, and then he nods. It's like he sees deep inside me and *knows*. He knows I need to express my gratitude in some way, and he lets me.

He goes into his bedroom to get ready for work, and when he comes back out, he's wearing jeans and a T-shirt. I dry my hands on a towel, and then he hands me what looks like a burner phone.

"I'll be at the shop, but you call or text me if you need anything. You'll be fine here. No one will mess with you." His jaw hardens as he says that last bit.

"Okay," I say.

He walks out of the door after one more glance at me.

I look down at the phone and see the number he's programmed into it. I see a note where he's added the name of the auto shop he works at and its address, and the thoughtfulness of his gesture gives me that warm, safe, cared-for feeling again.

Damon might just be a stranger I met in a bar last night, but he's proving to be more of a friend than I've ever had.

While he's gone, I remove the bandages from my feet and take a shower, standing under the hot spray for an extra long time like I'm trying to wash away every vestige of my old life. I soap up with Damon's body wash and shampoo, the same scent I recognized on him when he carried me inside last night.

I put the big T-shirt back on when I'm done and finger comb my long tresses as well as I can without a brush and then push it back over my shoulders to air dry. I don't have a toothbrush of my own yet, so I brush my teeth as best as I can with my finger and some of Damon's toothpaste. It seems too invasive for me to use his toothbrush without his permission, and I blush just at the thought of doing so. I've already invaded so much of the poor man's life.

My feet still sting a bit as I pad barefoot across the hardwood floor of Damon's apartment, but they aren't bleeding anymore, so I ignore the pain as I do what little I can to straighten up and clean for him.

His place isn't very strolled or dirty, but I find a duster and dust every surface I can find before I clean the windows and then sweep and mop the floors. His decor is masculine and bordering on spartan. There aren't any knick-knacks to dust around. Everything is minimalistic and functional. I've thoroughly cleaned everything way too soon, with the exception of his bedroom. I don't want to invade his privacy by entering his personal space without his knowledge.

I can't stand sitting here doing nothing, though. I should be out looking for a job and trying to get my new life off the ground, but I realize there's nothing I can do with no clothes, so I finally settle in on his couch and grab the remote, flicking the TV on to some cooking show.

I mindlessly watch it for a while, not really paying attention, too lost in my thoughts, until my eyelids begin to slip closed.

CHAPTER THREE

Damon

WHEN I COME HOME, my nostrils are assaulted by a clean, lemony scent. I look down and see that my floors have been mopped, and I notice there's not a speck of dust on any surface. My lips tip up in a grin. My little bunny has kept kept herself busy today.

I follow the sound of the TV into the living room and stop dead in my tracks, dropping the bags in my hands to the floor, my eyes roving over the delectable sight before me, my cock instantly at full mast, pushing painfully against the zipper of my jeans.

Christ. Hadley is laying curled on her side on my

couch with her head facing away from the TV. Her silky hair is hanging down, falling off the front of the cushions, and her little hands are pulled up under her chin in an angelic pose as she sleeps softly, but what has my dick about to bust my zipper are the rounded globes of her ass peeking out from beneath my shirt that has ridden up high on her thighs in her sleep.

It's the most perfect little ass I've ever seen in my life, and I ball my fists together to keep myself from going over to her and thrusting my cock between her cheeks. I want to slide between those perfect globes until I come all over her and smear it all over her ass, painting her as mine. Fuck her in *my* shirt, on *my* couch, in *my* apartment. *Mine, mine, mine.*

Fuck. I grit my teeth and force myself to walk away from her, leaving her innocently sleeping form undisturbed. I go into my bathroom, turn on the shower, strip down and then get under the spray, desperately jerking my swollen cock while thinking of all the filthy things I want to do to her. I'm so hard up for her, it only takes a few pumps until my breath catches and I'm blasting my spend all over the tiles.

I've thought about her nonstop all day while I worked on cars. I couldn't wait to get back home to her presence, but I never expected to find her the way she was.

I can't get the image of her plump little ass out of my mind. I want to hold it in my palms and mold it to my touch, slide my fingers between her sweet thighs into her dripping wet cunt until she comes all over them. Despite the fact that I just came harder than I ever have in my entire life, my fucking cock is hardening again.

Living with her and not touching her is going to be the death of me.

———

Hadley

I sit up on the couch and stretch languorously, wondering what time it is and how long I've been asleep. I can't believe I even fell asleep. I never fall asleep in the middle of the day.

I stop mid-yawn when I see the bags laying on the floor. Those weren't there when I fell asleep. I know because I cleaned the entire apartment before I dozed off while watching TV for lack of anything else to do.

Just then, Damon walks into the room from his bedroom, and my mouth goes dry at the sight of him.

He's wearing dark gray sweatpants and no shirt, and my question about whether he has ink on his chest too is finally answered. His entire right pec is covered by an abstract design that goes up to break at his shoulder before continuing on down his entire sleeve. Both of his arms are completely tatted, and he's nothing but hardened muscle. There's not an ounce of fat on him, though the slabs that are his abs are humongous. He's wearing the thick, braided silver chain and leather necklace, and I notice that the short hair on his head is glistening like he just got out of the shower. How did he come in without me even waking up?

My cheeks heat when my eyes finally travel up to meet his. His gray eyes are regarding me humorously, and I realize he's caught me staring at him.

"Hi," my voice comes out breathy. "How was your day?"

He leans down and picks up the bags before walking over to sit beside me on the couch. I'm surrounded by his scent as he sits mere inches from me and hands me the bags. "It was fine," he says, "I picked you up some things after work. I hope this is enough to get you started."

I peek into the bags, and at a glance, I see a toothbrush, rose-scented shampoo and conditioner, a hairbrush and hairdryer, leggings, tank tops, a pair of flip flops, and a pack of sports bras and cotton panties. I blush at the thought of him picking out my underthings.

"I didn't know your exact size, so I just got those universal sizes," he said gruffly. "Figured you're a small?"

I nod, imagining this big man picking out such tiny women's clothes. The thought makes me smile. "This is more than enough. Thank you."

He grunts by way of acknowledgement, and I look up to find his eyes on my bare thighs. I instinctively pull his shirt that I'm wearing down, and his jaw flexes before his gaze flicks down to my feet and he frowns. "Where are your bandages?"

"I had to take them off to take a shower this morning," I say.

"Stay there," he orders me. "I'll be right back."

He walks out of the room, and a moment later, he reappears with a wet washrag, a hand towel flung over his shoulder, and the salve and bandages.

"You don't have to do that," I begin to protest. "It's fine. I walked on them all day."

He silences me with a stern look before he says. "You've got open cuts. We don't want them to get infected." Then, just like last night, he proceeds to gently clean my feet before applying the salve and rewrapping them.

His hands linger on my ankles a moment before he finally pulls back and looks up at me, his gray eyes piercing me with their intensity. They're like the gray sky on a cloudy day, rolling and full of the threat of turbulence.

"Why don't you go change into some things that fit you?" he suggests, his voice gravelly. "Then, we'll see about doing something for dinner."

"Okay," I get up on shaky legs and go to do as he says, feeling the heat of his gaze on my back as I do so.

* * *

Damon

She's so fucking gorgeous it hurts. I inwardly curse myself when she comes out of her bedroom wearing a pair of tiny gray sleep shorts and a pink tank top. I can see the straps of the gray sports bra peeking out from under the straps of the tank top, and I know she's wearing a pair of the cotton panties I picked out for her. The pack I'd picked up for her was simple, but the fuckers had cute little designs printed on them of cherries, strawberries, and other fucking fruit, as if to entice a man to taste the sweetness between her legs.

I tried to buy the least sexy shit in the store

without being too obvious about it. I certainly couldn't have brought home a bag full of the lacy, silky lingerie I'd been tempted to buy for her. There's no way I'd be able to resist ripping that kind of stuff off her, but I'm beginning to think I could drape her in a burlap sack and she'd still be sex on legs.

And how the hell that is even possible when I'd bet my right hand she's never had sex before is beyond me. I don't know what it is about her, the innocence in her eyes, the ways she blushes too easily, but I'd be willing to bet she's still got that little cherry between her legs.

The thought pleases me immensely and causes a wave of lust to crash through me. I don't want to imagine another fucker ever touching her. Nobody else deserves her. Hell, I don't deserve her. She's a goddess too good for this world, too good for the likes of me.

That doesn't stop my body's reaction to her.

My cock twitches, but I fight to keep it from making an obscene tent in my pants. *Down boy.*

"What do you think about pizza?" I ask her.

She smiles a wide, girlish smile. "With pepperoni?"

I grin back at her, glad to have pleased her. "You got it."

I pick up my phone to place the order while she

sits on the couch and pulls her feet up underneath her, crosslegged.

"It won't be long," I tell her when I hang up the phone. "Tony's is located right next to the shop, and it's only about a five-minute drive from here."

"So you're a mechanic?" she asks me.

I shrug. "I work on cars, yeah."

"How long have you done that?" she asks curiously.

"About six months," I answer her honestly.

She looks surprised. "Oh, what did you do before then?"

I pause, looking into her innocent blue eyes. She has no idea what she's just asked me, and I consider dodging the question, but my conscience gets the better of me. She has a right to know the kind of man she's living with. "I was in prison," I admit, my voice coming out more gruffly than I intend.

I'm halfway expecting her to back away from me in fear or to just get up and leave, but she just looks at me. She doesn't even blink.

"Oh," she finally says, "I'm sorry."

My brow furrows, not sure I've heard her right. "What? What are you sorry for?"

She's regarding me frankly. "I didn't mean to pry.

I'm sorry if I asked you something you don't want to talk about."

I bark out an incredulous laugh and run my thumb along my jawline. "I admit to being a felon, and you're the one who's sorry. Sweetheart, I should be the one apologizing to you."

Now her little brow furrows, and her lips purse adorably. "What for?"

"I let you move in here without telling you what kind of man I am upfront."

When she doesn't say anything, I frown and add, "A criminal."

"You won't hurt me," she whispers, "so it doesn't matter."

"How do you know that?" my voice is low. She's right. I'd rather cut off my own hand than hurt her, but I'm half pissed at her for blindly trusting someone like me without knowing all the facts.

"You've had plenty of opportunity," she answers, "and you've been nothing but nice to me. Nicer than anyone has ever been." She whispers that last bit, and I can't help it. I reach out to cup her chin and raise her eyes up to me.

"I would never hurt you," I confirm, looking right into her eyes as I say it.

"I know," she says before her tongue darts out to wet her lips. My eyes are drawn to her full, puffy bottom lip, glistening with moisture. I feel my head drawing closer to her until my lips are only a hair's breath away from hers. Her breath hitches, but before I can taste her lips, there's a loud knock on the door that breaks me out of her siren call.

I get up to go get the pizza and tip the guy—though I probably shouldn't considering the moment he just killed—before heading back to the couch with the pizza box and a couple of cans of soda in tow.

"Dig in," I tell her as I set the box on the coffee table.

She grabs a slice, takes a bite, closes her eyes, and moans. *Christ*, does she always have to eat food like she's having sex? If she makes those sounds when she's eating, I can only imagine what kinds of noises she'd make with me in between her thighs.

"Possession with intent to distribute," I tell her.

"What?" she asks, stopping mid-bite.

"What I was in for," I explain.

She shakes her head. "I didn't ask."

"I know," I tell her, "but I think you have a right to know."

She nods slowly before asking me, "Did you know what you were doing?"

My chest constricts. No one's ever asked me that

before. They just hear my charge and assume I'm a piece of shit drug dealer.

But not this sweet girl. She gives me the benefit of the doubt. She sees me for the man I really am, the man I was before all the shit hit the fan that night five years ago. If I wasn't obsessed with her before, I sure as hell am now.

I shake my head, "No. I didn't know what I was transporting. I knew I was working with shady people. The money was too good for me to assume otherwise, but no, I had no idea what I was holding when I got busted."

I still remember it like it was yesterday. I went to drop off the package and out of nowhere was surrounded by a slew of FBI agents.

They'd tried to offer me a deal—immunity to snitch on who I worked for, but I knew better. I'd kept my trap shut and been lucky to get off with five years in the pen. I haven't gone near that crowd since I got out of prison. Back when I got tangled up with them, I was a stupid kid from the wrong side of the tracks, so when they approached me with an easy gig, I took. No questions asked.

After I got out of prison, though, I got the job at Rick's garage. Rick and I grew up together, and when he found out what had happened to me, he was there ready to help. He knows the kind of guy I am. He was the only one in the city to give a felon a chance. He's the closest thing I've ever had to a true friend.

She nods. "I believe you."

My chest swells at those three little words. She believes me. No questions asked. She trusts me.

She's an angel.

I watch her take another bite of her pizza. She closes her eyes and moans again, and I fight back a grin. The girl really enjoys her food.

I'll feed her whatever she wants every day. I'll do anything to keep her safe and happy.

She's *my* angel, and I'm going to take care of her.

CHAPTER FOUR

Hadley

DAMON LETS me ride with him to the auto shop he works at the next day. He tells me to go next door to apply to Tony's for a job, that he's pretty sure they're hiring.

I'm thrilled when I'm hired right on the spot. It's not a super fancy joint, but it's not a total dive either. They sell more than just pizza. It's more of an Italian restaurant than just a pizzeria. I spend the entire day training, and after work Damon takes me shopping so I can pick up the appropriate type of clothes for the job.

I need a white button-up shirt, black pants, and some black shoes since that's what they want their waitresses to wear there. I grab a few white camis and bras too since I can't wear the colorful sports bras Damon bought me underneath a white button-up.

Damon gives me a wad of cash and waits outside the store on one of the mall's benches, giving me my privacy. The bench is facing the store, though, and every time I look up, his eyes are watching me and flicking around the store, taking in everyone coming and going. It makes me feel safe, like he's guarding me.

When I finish, he drives us back to his apartment where we both take showers, and then we wind up watching TV together on the couch while eating turkey sandwiches.

And that's the routine we fall into. I ride with Damon to work every day. It's perfect since I work right next to him. He comes over and eats lunch at the diner, and he always leaves me tips that are way too generous. More often than not, I take my lunch break when he's there and eat lunch with him. That way I keep him from giving me humongous tips that I don't deserve.

True to my word, when I get my first paycheck, I pay him back for all the clothes and necessities he bought me. He acts like he doesn't really want to take it, but when I insist, he does. When I offer to pay for half the rent, that's when he puts his foot down. He tells me he'd be paying the same amount regardless of whether I lived there or not, so I finally let it go, recognizing that it's a battle I won't win.

I'm happier than I can ever remember being in my whole life. I have a job and a place to live where I feel safe, and Damon is nothing short of amazing to me.

I realize that I'm probably becoming too attached to him. Sometimes when I look at him, I get this tickly feeling deep in my tummy, especially when he smiles at me or when he's walking around bare-chested with all his tats and muscles showing.

Sometimes I wonder what it would be like for him to kiss me. I thought he was going to that day we were sitting on the couch together and he told me he'd been in prison, but then the pizza guy had shown up, and I figured I must have just imagined it all since he hasn't so much as laid a finger on me since then.

He's been respectfully distant. A true gentleman. The closet Damon comes to touching me is with his eyes that seem to caress every inch of me, but that's probably just my wishful imagination too.

Damon is my friend and roommate and nothing more.

And really that's probably for the best. We don't need to complicate things since we're living together.

I'm just grateful for the break I've been given after running away from home in the middle of the night after what my stepdad tried to do. I shudder remembering his body on top of mine. I realize things could have turned out very differently for me that night if I'd run into someone besides Damon. Damon might be a felon, but he's the most honorable man I've ever known.

I know I'm safe with him.

* * *

Damon

It's the sweetest torture being around her so much and denying myself, but it's worth it. *She's* worth it.

I tell myself day after day that this is enough. Sitting on the couch with her after work and watching a movie together. Eating lunch together. Riding to and from work together. Seeing the way her nipples pebble when she gets chilled while we're watching movie. Those goddamned sports bras I bought her don't do anything to hide them.

I made sure she got a job at Tony's. Fortunately, I know Tony. He went to school with Rick and me, and he was more than willing to take her on after I put in a good word for her.

I'd have been okay with her not working and staying here in my apartment where I knew she was safe, but there was no way Hadley would have ever gone for that. She has this fierce desire to prove herself and make her own way as much as she can, and I have to respect that—no matter how tempted I might be to lock her up and never let her leave.

There was no way in hell I was going to chance her getting a job across town where I wouldn't be able to check on her as often as I want. Although I drop by Tony's every day for lunch, she has no idea how many times throughout the day I also walk by to glance in the window at her and make sure she's okay.

I realize I'm completely fucking obsessed with her, but god help me. I can't stop. I need to look at her a hundred times a day—at least.

My entire apartment smells of her. The scent of the rose shampoo I bought her follows her everywhere and clings to every surface. I jack off every night with her scent in my lungs and the vision of her sweet face in my mind.

And that's just it. I don't even have to picture her body to come. I can come just remembering her smile or her laugh. Fuck, everything about her has me ready to blow at a moment's notice.

She's reduced me to a goddamn animal through no fault of her own. No, she's so damn innocent she doesn't have a clue what she's doing to me.

And fuck if that doesn't make me want her even more.

She's the light inside my darkness, the sunshine that brings warmth to my dreary world.

I mean it. Even if she never wants to be anything more than friends with me, I have to have her in my life. She's like a drug that I'm addicted to. Every glance at her is a hit that sends a high throughout my system.

Of course, I know it's selfish, but I know there's no way I'll ever be able to let her be with another man. It would destroy me if she let another man touch her.

Not that I touch her. I've been careful *not* to touch her because I'm afraid that with my growing obsession if I do I'll lose control and won't be able to stop.

I content myself with drinking in every bright smile she throws my way, every ripple of her hair, how she chews on her bottom lip when she's in deep thought, the sexy little moans she makes when she's eating something she really likes.

I'd do anything for her.

That's why when I suddenly hear screams coming from her bedroom, I'm up in a flash, my heart pounding in my chest and rushing to her room.

"Hadley!" I burst into her room, my eyes flicking all around the dim area, checking for any threat or danger before I see her small form thrashing in the bed. Her eyes are closed. She's in the throes of a nightmare.

She screams again, and I hurry to her side, sitting on the edge of her bed and leaning over her to grip her shoulders and pull her up, gently shaking her to try to awaken her from whatever hell she's reliving.

Her panicked eyes flutter open. Her breathing is ragged as she stares up at me unseeingly. "It's just a nightmare." I pet the side of her hair soothingly and my god, her raven tresses are just as silky as I imagined.

"Damon?" she speaks my name, and the wobbly, choked way she says it is like a punch to my gut.

Tears form in her eyes, and in the next instant, she launches herself at me, her arms clinging tight around me, burrowing her head in the crook of my neck.

I allow her to crawl onto my lap where I settle her sitting sideways, loving the way she clings to me, looking for protection and solace.

"Ssh," I murmur against her hair, stroking my

hands gently up and down her back like I'd pet a frightened kitten, "I've got you, sweetheart."

Her tears wet my chest as she cries against me, but eventually she quiets and stops trembling.

I'm hyperaware of the curve of her ass sitting in my lap, and I don't see how she can't feel my hard-on. I feel like an ass for getting hard right now when I'm just supposed to be comforting her, but I'm a man goddammit, and she feels so soft and warm in my arms.

I feel the featherlight pressure of petal-soft lips against my neck and jump like I've been electrocuted. Christ, she *kissed* me.

I pull roughly back from her and look down into her blue eyes that are still watery from her tears, and I begin drowning. "Hadley," my voice comes out strangled.

She moves her hand up to cup my face, and I see her hand shake as she lifts it. When her palm meets my cheek, I turn into it like an affection-starved dog, closing my eyes and reveling in her touch.

"Damon," she says my name all breathy, and my arms tighten around her, my control waning thin. It's taking everything within me not to lay her back on the bed and fucking ravish her.

I start to pull back from her, but she clambers to sit upright on me, straddling me with her sweet thighs draped around me, her pussy sitting right on the bulge I *know* she has to feel, nothing separating our sexes but my sweatpants and her short pajama shorts.

God, what I want to do to her. But she just had a nightmare, and I can't take advantage of her like this. I can't.

I start to move her off me, but her arms tighten around my neck and she whimpers, "Don't you want me?" She wiggles innocently on my bulge, and I groan.

"You don't know what you're asking me, Hadley." My voice is dark and strained with the effort it takes me not to crush her to me.

She hesitates a moment, looking unsure of herself, before she leans forward and presses her lips to mine.

It's a soft, chaste kiss, just the barest brush of her puffy lips against mine. Shit, I don't think the girl has ever even been kissed before, and the thought that she might want me to be her first kiss detonates something off inside me.

I grasp the back of her neck, anchoring her to me as I crush my lips against her. I suck at her bottom lip, eliciting a gasp from her, and I take advantage of the opportunity to slide my tongue into her mouth, seeking out her own tongue. She tastes sweet, like berries, tearing a moan from deep within my soul.

She mewls into my mouth and melts against me,

sending fire licking through my veins. My suspicion that she's never been kissed before is confirmed when her tongue tentatively moves against mine in an unpracticed rhythm, but that's okay because I'm more than happy to teach her and lead her in the dance.

I can't fucking think. All I can do is taste. I'm running off primal energy. With one hand still behind her head, I move the other to her waist and hold her as I lift my hips, pressing my hardness up against her softness.

She whimpers, and I somehow manage to tear my lips from her, leaning back to put some distance between our chests.

Fuck, I can see her hard little nipples through her tank top and the thin sports bra. Her lips are wet and swollen, her hair falling around her shoulders in dark, messy waves. Her eyes are sinfully lidded at half mast until they go wide as she looks up at me with such a look of stunned, curious innocence that I don't know whether to laugh or weep.

"Did I do something wrong?" she asks.

I bark out an incredulous laugh. "Fuck, no, sweetheart."

When she continues to look up at me, endearingly worried and self-conscious, I run a finger along the side of her flawless cheek. "You're perfect," I tell her honestly. "Why would you think you did anything wrong?"

Her cheeks color, "Because I've never..." she trails off, her eyes glancing away from me.

Fuck, I've already figured out she's a virgin but to hear the confirmation from her own lips...

I try to set her mind at ease. "You have nothing to worry about, Hadley. I would never take advantage of you."

She chews on her bottom lip for a moment before she whispers, "What if I want you to?"

I make a strangled sound, every muscle in my goddamn body tensing. The beast inside me is snarling to come out. She's unknowingly baiting him and working him into a frenzy.

"You can't say things like that to me, Hadley," I croak out, pulling her closer to me against my good sense. It's dangerous to hold her like this when my control is so close to snapping, but god, she feels good. So good.

"Why not?" her question is little more than a whisper.

"Because if I lose control with you, that's it. I'll never be able to stop, sweetheart." My eyes blaze down into hers, trying to communicate with her just how serious I am. If I fuck her now, she's mine. There will be no going back. Ever.

I don't know what the fuck is wrong with me, why I'm holding back. This is everything I want. Hadley is basically offering herself to me.

Maybe it's because I'm afraid she's offering me one night out of the curiosity of a virgin who needs comforting, and I know that will never be enough for me. She's already under my skin, but once I get inside her, it'll be game over. She'll be mine whether she likes it or not.

She reaches out and skims shaky fingers over my chest, causing all my muscles to bunch and ripple.

I grab her hand, capturing it in my own, and she looks up at me with a gasp. "You're playing with fire, little girl," I warn her.

She continues to gaze up at me with those fuck-me eyes, and I feel like I can't breathe. I'm surrounded by her scent, painfully aware of the heat where our bodies touch, and I'm trying to remind myself of why I'm so careful around her. She's my angel, and I'd never do anything to hurt her or scare her. I need to keep her safe from everything—including me.

But what she says next shreds the tattered remains of my reasoning.

"Then burn me."
And I lose it.
I *fucking* lose it.
Game on.

CHAPTER FIVE

Hadley

A DEEP SHUDDER passes throughout Damon's body before he hauls me back against his chest and claims my lips again.

Instead of the crash I'm expecting, he's surprisingly gentle this time, his kiss languid as he teases my lips, his tongue playing a game of hide and seek with my own as he flits it in and out of my mouth.

His hands are everywhere all at once. Running through my hair, down the sides of my neck, over my collarbone, down my arms, gripping my ass and pulling me tighter against that swollen part of him at the apex of his thighs.

When his lips finally move from mine, they lick and suck and taste my jaw, behind my ears, my neck, my shoulders.

I'm flooded with sensation, and all I can do is whimper and mewl my pleasure.

I've never been kissed before, but if it feels like this, then no wonder people do it. Something tells me that it doesn't feel like this for everyone, though. This is special because it's Damon. Me and Damon.

He takes deep inhales near my neck like he's trying to breathe me in, and something about that causes wetness to pool between my legs.

There's an ache there, an insistent throbbing that I've never felt before, and I move on instinct, rubbing myself against Damon's hardness, seeking to alleviate that ache. Tickles of pleasure snap between my legs when I rock against his bulge, and he hisses in a sharp breath, grabbing hold of my waist to anchor me against him and keep me still.

"You keep dragging that dripping wet little virgin pussy all over my cock, I'm not gonna make it, sweetheart," Damon growls against my lips.

His words are coarse and filthy, but that only

makes me throb even more as more wetness gathers between my thighs.

"Damon," I plead in a whine, though I'm not exactly sure what I'm pleading for. I just want more. More of this. More of him.

I had a nightmare about my stepfather, but when I woke up to Damon comforting me, I wanted nothing more than to just stay in his arms forever—this big, muscled, tatted felon who most people would be frightened of at one glance but who's the only person I've ever really felt safe with.

Damon's the only one I would ever trust to take my virginity. And I desperately want him to right now. He makes me feel safe and wanted and beautiful.

He nips down on my shoulder with his teeth, and then he licks where he bit, soothing the sting away with his worshipping tongue. Something about it is so carnal, so animalistic that is causes something to curl deep within my belly.

His hands are skimming over my bare stomach as he raises my tank top up, his thumbs hooking under the bottom of the sports bra to drag it up with the shirt as he pulls them off over the top of my head, baring my hardened nipples to his hungry gaze.

He lightly strokes the pad of his thumb over one, eliciting a sharp moan from me. It's like a wire is connecting my nipple to the throb between my legs because I get impossibly wetter.

"Jesus, Hadley," he murmurs darkly, "I can feel your wetness soaking through my sweatpants, you beautiful, perfect, horny little virgin."

I would be embarrassed by the wetness there were it not for the fact that Damon seems to really like it.

One of his hands moves down between us to stroke me through the fabric while he moves his mouth down to lick the sensitive nub of one of my nipples.

The double sensation has me arching my back and gasping out a moan, and then the next thing I know I'm turning in mid-air as he holds me up in his arms and flips me until I'm laying flat on the bed again.

He hovers over me, looking like a dark angel, his gray eyes dark and stormy.

He kisses his way down my stomach to the band of my shorts before he pulls them down my trembling legs.

I instinctively start to close my legs, suddenly shy, but he pushes his shoulders between them and holds them open with a palm on each of my thighs.

"Fuck me," he says lowly as he stares down at that most intimate part of me. "This is the most beautiful little pussy I've ever seen, sweetheart."

He reaches out a finger and slides it up and down

my wet slit reverently. The feeling of his bare skin touching me *there* has every one of my nerve endings snapping and crackling. My breathing starts coming in short gasps when he finds a little button and begins to circle it with the pad of his thumb, sending little jolts of pleasure throughout my core.

I feel his breath pass over me there as he studies what he's doing, and then his tongue snakes out to replace his thumb, and I scream at the electricity that jolts through me, my legs shaking.

"Goddamn," he groans before he begins to lick and suck me in earnest, lapping at me like he's on death row and I'm his last meal.

"Damon," I whimper his name and wiggle beneath him, trying to pull away, trying to get closer. Hell, I don't know what I'm trying to do, only that the pleasure is so intense I can't sit still, but Damon drapes a heavy arm over my stomach, trapping me in place, and then I feel pressure between my legs as he slowly slips a finger into me.

I tense, but then Damon soothes me with a low, "Relax, I'm going to make you feel so good, pretty baby," spoken right against my sensitive nub before he starts licking and sucking it again.

He strokes his finger slowly in and out, and I gradually relax as I get used to the feeling. Then, he adds another finger, and I feel impossibly full. But he keeps licking and sucking on my little nub, sending spikes of pleasure racing throughout me.

I feel like my body is climbing toward something. A pressure is building inside me, and I'm nearly sobbing as I plead with him, "Damon, please."

He smirks up at me before he latches onto the little nub, sucking harder, unrelentingly, as his fingers curve up and rub against this spot inside me, and then I explode with a sharp cry that takes my breath away.

My whole body feels like it's convulsing, and then I'm floating, my limbs waxen.

"Fuck, fuck, fuck," he chants as his sits up, quickly slipping his sweatpants off to reveal his massive cock. It's thick and swollen and angry-looking, and my eyes widen. I don't see how it can possibly fit in me.

"Gotta have you, sweetheart," he tells me as he lines it up with my pussy, rubbing the head up and down against my lips, coating it in wetness.

I barely have a moment to marvel at how something so hard could feel so velvety smooth against me before I feel an insistent, burning pressure as he starts slipping it inside me.

"Damon," I whine his name in a half plea, half something I don't know.

"Ssh," he quiets me as he strokes my hair, still

pushing slowly in. "You'll adjust to me. I promise, baby, and I'll go slow."

I whimper, and he leans over me, gathering me to his chest with his arms behind my back, holding me close to him as he continues to slowly push.

He finally stops, and his arms are taut around me. He pulls back just enough to look into my eyes. His eyes are dark with lust, but his voice is filled with adoration as he rains praises down on me, "Good girl, beautiful girl, my sweet angel…"

I bask in his praise and feel myself relaxing, but then he pulls back and pushes hard, breaking through my barrier of innocence, and I scream.

He swallows my scream with his mouth, kissing me gently, his tongue apologizing to me as it dances with mine.

He doesn't move that part of him as he licks at my lips, giving me time to adjust to him. "You okay, sweetheart?" He asks me when he finally pulls back from my lips.

I draw in a shaky breath and realize that the pain has subsided, and now there's just a dull ache there. I nod, but he still doesn't move. Every muscle in his body seems to be tense, and his jaw hardens with the effort of holding himself back.

I wiggle beneath him, causing him to slide within

me, and he lets out a deep, guttural groan, his head falling down as if he's in pain.

"Fuck, Hadley, I can't stay still, baby. Gotta move," he tells me as he starts pulling that huge part of himself out and then shoving it back inside me. He pulls more and more out each time, slamming more back in, and the wet friction of his sex rubbing into mine causes a deeper kind of pressure to start building inside me.

I moan at the sensation and arch my back up into him, wrapping my arms and legs around him.

"Fuck, yes, hold onto me, baby," he groans into my ear as he picks up his pace until he's stroking his full length in and out of me.

"Fuck, you're mine, aren't you, sweetheart?" he's panting into my ear. "This is my pussy, isn't it? It was fucking made for me, wasn't it? It's sucking and gripping me so tight, just begging me to bust up in it and mark it as mine, isn't it?"

I'm mewling and moaning right along with him, the filth of his words shamelessly turning me on even more, the pressure building and building until I'm crying out his name as waves of sensation crash over me.

"Damon!" I scream his name when the tidal wave hits me, my sex convulsing around him.

His breath catches, and his hands move to cup my

ass as he continues to saw himself in and out of me, riding me through the waves. "That's it. Open for me, baby," he tells me, pumping into me faster now.

Sweat glistens on his skin, and his gray eyes blaze wildly down at me as he groans, "Fuck, Hadley, fuck! You're mine!"

His possessive words send another ripple of pleasure through me, and I feel myself clenching up again.

He roars and then leans down to bite down on my shoulder savagely as he thrusts into me one last time and stills, holding himself deep.

I feel his hard length swelling before it bursts and pulses, his hot liquid pouring into me.

The hard muscles of his back ripple under my fingertips where I'm still clinging to him, and then he falls onto his side, scooping me up and pulling me with him.

He's still seated deep within me as he gathers me close to his chest and places a kiss on my forehead, whispering, "Mine," against my skin.

Yours, I want to tell him, but I'm too tired, too weak in the aftermath of our passion. I feel my eyes close, and I burrow my head against his chest as I succumb to the pull of sleep.

Damon

I don't sleep. I can't. I hold Hadley and stroke her hair. She's a sleeping angel in my arms.

And she's mine. Fucking *mine*. My dick starts to harden again just thinking about how she gave herself to me so perfectly, how she came all over my cock, her soft little mewls and pants in my ear.

Being inside her was even more incredible than I imagined. It was like being joined to the other half of my soul. I'm so much bigger than her. She's so goddamned tiny, yet somehow she fits me perfectly.

I continue to pet her, my little sex kitten. I drink in the sight of her like a man starved for water. Her dark lashes lay against her porcelain skin. Her lips are red and swollen from my kisses. They're slightly parted as she sleeps softly.

I want to sink into her again, but there's no way I'm going to wake her when she's sleeping so peacefully.

Plus, she's probably sore after her first time. I wasn't exactly gentle there near the end. I'm sure she'll need time to recover. I'm not a small man by any means.

Claiming her changes everything and nothing. I'll still do anything for her, but it's like everything has been amplified times a million.

I was protective of her before, but add possessive on top of that now. I'm like a wild animal that's found his mate and wants to stay glued next to her side at all times to ensure no one fucks with what's his.

Jesus, I hope I don't terrify her with my intensity, but I can't help it. I tried to fucking tell her, but she asked for it, practically begged me for it, rubbing that sweet little cunt all over me.

As if she can feel my thoughts on her, she stirs in my arms and slowly blinks her eyes open.

When she sees me gazing down at her, she smiles shyly.

"Hi," she says breathily.

"Hey, sweetheart," my voice is so soft and tender I almost don't recognize it, but I don't give a fuck because that's what she does to me.

"This is nice," she says, burrowing closer to my chest.

I chuckle. "Glad you think so because I'm going to hold you like this every night from here on out, honey. You're mine now, and I'm not going anywhere."

I look down into her crystal blue eyes to try to gauge the impact my statement has on her, but I see nothing but contentment in her eyes. Thank Jesus.

"Promise?" she asks me, her expression trusting and hopeful, and my heart about bursts out of my chest. I'm thanking my lucky stars that this beautiful, perfect girl wants me. I don't know what the fuck I did to deserve her, but I'm going to spend every day for the rest of my life trying to be good enough for her.

"You're goddamn right I promise," I tell her. "Satan himself couldn't drag me away from you, baby." I'd fight the devil and all his demons, brave a nuclear bomb, go to hell and back, all just for the *chance* to be with her.

She smiles up at me, the perfect picture of innocence. She's the only thing that's right about this broken world.

And now that I've got her in my arms right where she belongs, I'm never letting go.

CHAPTER SIX

Hadley

I'M SO DELIRIOUSLY HAPPY. Damon held me all night after he took me for the first time. Yes, there was a pinch of pain when he shredded my innocence, but after that, there was nothing but pleasure.

Such intense pleasure...

I wondered if he was going to take me again, but he didn't. When I looked up at him expectantly this morning, he groaned and told me to stop looking at him like that, that as much as he wanted to sink into me again my body needed to rest.

I feel the twinge of soreness between my thighs

and suppose he's right. He's just as large down *there* as he is everywhere else, and I *am* sore.

Deliciously sore. I welcome the soreness because it reminds me of how thoroughly he claimed me, how he possessively called me *his*.

I want to be his. I need to be his.

He just holds me, stroking his hands all down my hair and back and arms, petting me like I'm a favored pet. And I love every minute of it. I love being held by him. I love how big he is around me. It makes me feel safe.

When he drops me off at work, he gives me a smoldering kiss that makes my knees so weak they wobble when I stand to walk into the restaurant. He grins at me crookedly like he knows exactly what he does to me before reminding me that he's right next door if I need anything.

My shift has barely begun and I already can't wait for it to be over with so we can go home and I can be in his arms again.

Thankfully, my work at the diner always goes by quickly. I stay busy waiting tables, and the constant shuffle back and forth makes time fly.

Everything's going great until I walk out of the kitchen and over to my section and stop dead in my tracks when I see who's sitting in a booth by himself.

It's my stepfather.

My heart rate ticks up, and my palms feel sweaty. I feel that fight or flight instinct rising within me, and just as I'm contemplating running, I see that there's no use because his eyes are trained right on me.

"Hadley." The way he says my name makes my skin crawl.

I take a deep breath and try to tell myself that I'm safe here. We're in public, and he wouldn't try anything in public with so many people around.

I square my shoulders and take the next couple of steps over to his table. "What can I get for you?" I ask him, pulling out my pad and pen, treating him just like he's any other customer.

As much as the thought of serving him anything grates on my nerves, I can't make a scene and risk losing this job. Not when everything is finally going so good for me and my life is looking up. I won't let him take this away from me.

How did he even get here, though? He's never taken my mom or me out to eat here. I didn't even know the place existed until Damon told me about it.

Of course, I shouldn't be so shocked that Randal knows about places we don't. There's no telling what kind of secret life he's led outside the house all these years. My mom stays home high all the time, and I'd rather suck lemons that go anywhere with Randal, so if he went out, of course he went out alone.

Just my luck, though, that he ends up in the one restaurant I happen to work at.

He tsks under his breath as he looks at me, and then his eyes sweep up and down my frame, openly appraising me in my work uniform. I'm completely covered in the black slacks and white button-up top, my hair swept back from my face in a ponytail, but the way he's looking at me makes me feel like I have nothing on.

"What you can do is come back home," he tells me frankly. "Your mother has been worried sick about you."

I doubt that Mom has even been lucid enough to know I'm gone, much less to worry about me.

I don't say that, though. Instead, I shake my head at Randal. "No, I have a new life now. I'm happy where I'm at."

Randal's jaw hardens as he looks up at me. "You'll bring your ass back home where you belong, or I'll drag you there by that goddamned ponytail."

I take an instinctive step back from him. "I'm eighteen now. You can't make me go anywhere with you if I don't want to," I say more bravely than I feel.

His hand snatches out to grab my wrist so fast I

don't have time to move back until he's already got me held fast in his hard grip.

I can't help the strangled cry that leaves my lips at the painful pressure. It's like he's trying to break my wrist, but the next thing I know a huge form is towering behind me.

"I think you'd better get your hands off her right now," Damon's voice is a predatory growl, and I feel my heart leap within me. He's here. Everything will be okay now. Damon won't let anything happen to me.

Randal narrows his eyes up at Damon, but he instantly releases my wrist. I pull it back to me and rub it with my hand, a motion that doesn't go unnoticed by Damon. Fire flashes in his eyes as he looks back at Randal again.

"I'm going to give you until the count of three to get out here, or I swear to God I'll break your worthless jaw."

"Who the fuck do you think—" Randal begins, but then Tony, the owner of the restaurant comes over. I look up and realize that every eye in the restaurant is on us.

"I'm not even giving you until the count of three. Get out." His head jerks toward the door, telling Randal exactly where to go.

Randal looks between the two men before his eyes

flit back to me accusingly. He *would* act like this is all my fault. That's just the type of asshole he is. Randal is the king of gaslighting. Nothing is ever his fault in his book.

He mutters something under his breath that I can't make out, but he heads for the door.

"Don't ever come back here," Tony calls after him. "No one manhandles my staff here."

Randal doesn't say anything as he exits, the little bell to the restaurant ringing in the dead silence as everyone watches.

My face heats at the stir we've caused, but then Tony splays his hands and grins, and everyone in the restaurant applauds like he's a hero before they get back to their meals.

Damon puts his hand on the small of my back and leads me to the back office area where we're joined by Tony a second later.

"You know that guy?" Tony asks me.

I nod before confessing. "Yeah, he's my stepdad."

Tony shoots a knowing glance over my head at Damon that lets me know Damon must have told him about Randal. While that might should anger me, it doesn't. Instead, I'm grateful that I don't have to explain it all again.

"Well, he won't be coming around here anymore,"

Tony assures me. "You want to take the rest of the day off?"

"What?" I ask in surprise before continuing. "No. No way. I'm fine. Really. I promise."

"Hadley," Damon begins, but I interrupt him.

"Damon, I'm fine. I won't let him get to me. I can finish my shift."

Damon's eyes flicker with something that I think is pride, and Tony looks pleasantly surprised as well.

Tony nods at me. "Okay, then, if you're sure you're okay."

"I am," I reiterate. I'm not going to let Randal make me look like I'm a weakling. I might have run from him once, but I'm safe here. I'm not going to let him run me out of my job—even if the manager did offer to let me have the rest of the day off.

"At least go ahead and take your break," Tony tells me.

"Okay," I concede to that.

Tony walks away and leaves me and Damon standing together.

Damon reaches out his hand and strokes it down my hair before cupping my cheek. "You sure you're okay, sweetheart?" His eyes look down at me with concern.

I take a deep breath and nod. "Yeah, I can't say it

wasn't disconcerting seeing him again, but you guys handled it." I smile up at him, but his jaw hardens as he thinks back on it.

"I should have snapped his neck," he grinds out.

I place my hand on his cheek now, and he covers it with his own hand. "Nobody touches you," he tells me, an almost feral light in his eyes.

"Nobody but you," I confirm to him, sensing that's what he needs to hear, and then his lips crash down on mine desperately.

He kisses me feverishly, leaving no doubt in my mind that this isn't just any kiss. This kiss is a claiming. He's possessively staking his claim on me, marking me with his lips, and that causes my knees to weaken.

He feels me slumping, and his arms go around me to pull me against him and hold me up.

I'm pressed flush against him, and I feel his hardness pressing against my stomach.

I boldly reach between us to grasp it, and he hisses in a breath.

"Goddamn, Hadley, are you trying to get fucked?"

My core clenches at his crass words. "Yes," I breath against his lips.

He groans and pulls back from me slightly, his brow furrowed. "Aren't you still sore, sweetheart?"

"I don't care," I tell him, throwing my arms around his neck and burrowing close to him again.

"Fuck," he groans into my hair, "I can't say no to you, baby doll."

He hoists me up, and my legs wrap around his waist. I feel his hardness pressing between my thighs, and I instinctively begin to gyrate against him, seeking that delicious friction that I know leads to intense pleasure.

He carries me into a room that must be Tony's private office and locks the door before thrusting my back up against it.

"Where are we?" I ask him. As badly as I want him, I don't want to get fired for letting my boyfriend fuck me in the manager's office.

"Tony's private office," he breaths in between kissing my neck. "Don't worry. Tony won't mind even if he finds out." He grins up at me wickedly as he undoes the buttons on my blouse, pushing one of the cups of my bra down and sucking a nipple into his mouth.

And then I stop caring one way or the other.

I arch against him, offering him my breasts, and he pays the same attention to the other one before he sets me down long enough to unbutton my pants and pull them off me. He doesn't bother with pulling my panties off. Instead he unzips his jeans, frees his cock, and then hoists me back up against the wall.

"Fuck, baby. I gotta get inside that sweet little pussy right now," he tells me before he roughly pulls my panties to the side and enters me in one swift thrust.

He captures my cry with his mouth, his tongue plunging in and out of my mouth to mirror the way he pistons his cock in and out of me.

"Fuck, am I hurting you, baby? I should slow down," It's like he's talking both to me and himself, trying to convince himself he needs to be gentler with me, but his body is out of control and doesn't want to listen.

"No," I moan against him. "Don't stop, please don't stop. Harder," I tell him. Though there's a twinge of pain, there's pleasure too, and all I can think about is more. More of this. More of him. I feel that little ball curling tighter and tighter in my belly, and when he drags himself in and out, he keeps hitting that spot that sends tingles of pleasure all throughout my body.

"Motherfucker," Damon groans against my neck, increasing the speed of his thrusts. The door is banging, and I don't see how anyone couldn't know what's going on behind this door if anyone comes back here.

"Fuck, baby, I need you to come," Damon's voice is

gravelly and desperate, and I can feel him swelling impossibly larger inside me. "Need to feel that little pussy fall open around me when I nut in you," he growls into my ear as he reaches between us and presses his thumb down on my clit.

His dirty talk and that one touch are enough to set me off. I bite my lip, drawing blood as I try to contain the shrill cry that tears throughout my entire being as I come hard. The sound that escapes my lips is strangled and harsh, something between the mix of a moan and a whimper, and I feel my muscles contract around him.

"Fuck, yeah, baby. Oh, here I come, honey, and it's all for you." Damon manages to croak in my ear before I feel the hard jets of his spend spraying deep within me, triggering another orgasm.

He buries his head in the crook of my neck to muffle the sound of his groans as he continues to ejaculate deep inside me while my pussy pulses all around him, milking every drop from his swollen member.

He holds me there for what seems like forever. Every muscle in my body is lax when he finally pulls out of me and then makes sure I can stand before he disappears into Tony's private bathroom and comes out with some wet paper towels.

I lean against the door in a daze as he gently cleans me up before he redresses me like I'm a favorite doll, pulling my pants back up me and then buttoning my shirt back up.

He leans in and presses his lips possessively against mine. "Mine," he whispers before he pulls back and removes the hair tie from my hair, running his fingers through my hair to straighten out where it became mussed and was falling out from where he'd roughly taken me against the door.

I finally get my wits about me enough to stand up straight, run my fingers through my hair, and gather it back up into a ponytail.

"I think break time is over," I say.

Damon chuckles before pressing his lips against my forehead. "Best damn break I ever had, sweetheart."

Me too, I think. *God, me too.*

CHAPTER SEVEN

Hadley

THE REST of my shift goes by without incident. Though I'm still a bit strung tight after what transpired with my stepfather earlier and find myself glancing over my shoulder more often than usual, I'm able to perform my job seamlessly enough, I think.

By the end of my shift, I'm finally starting to relax. I'll be going home with Damon soon, and I already can't wait to be in his arms again.

I open my locker at the back of the restaurant to retrieve my purse. I don't carry much with me. Just my wallet and a few necessities. Tony provides all of us girls with a tiny locker space where we can lock our purses and any other belongings up when we're working our shifts. He wants to eliminate the chance of any drama, such as a waitress losing her purse and crying that someone stole it. That's why he makes sure to provide us with the lockers.

I frown when a little slip of paper falls out of my locker. It's torn and looks like it was hastily ripped from another sheet.

I bend over to pick it up where it floated to the floor.

My hands begin to tremble when I read what's scrawled on it.

I know who you're living with. I know who is and what he was in prison for. If you don't want him to go back, you'll come home, and you'll never run away again.

How did Randal find all this out? Yeah, he saw Damon in the restaurant earlier when Damon threatened him, but how did he find out I was living with him? Better yet, how did he find out what he was in prison for? How did he get this note in here?

My blood freezes in my veins when I realize what he said. *If you don't want him to go back...* I don't like what that implies. Is Randal saying that he would frame Damon somehow just to get him locked back up?

I think back on everything I know about Randal. He might be a piece of shit, but he's actually friends with several cops. They're probably dirty cops. They'd have to be to be friends with Randal, right?

I look back down at the note, and my heart crumbles within me.

I close my eyes and absently drop the note into my purse.

I can't risk Damon getting locked back up because of me.

The tears start to roll down my face as I begin moving toward the back door of the restaurant to slip out the back where Damon can't see me. He always waits for me out front.

My heart breaks when I think of Damon waiting for me only for me to not show up. I think of the confusion that'll cloud his face. Will he think I just up and left him? As much as it hurts my heart to think that's what he'll conclude, that's what I need him to think. For his own safety.

At least I shouldn't have to worry about him coming after me. I never told him where I used to live, and I wrote his address on my application to Tony's so he won't know the address of my childhood home.

I stick to the back alleys as I slowly begin to make my way back to the block my mom and stepdad live on.

I swore I'd never go back there, but I'll break my promise to myself to save Damon, the man I now know I love without a shadow of a doubt.

Damon

Something's wrong. Hadley is never late coming off her shift. I wait exactly five minutes for in case she got held up in the bathroom or something before I barge through the restaurant and straight to the employee section in the back.

When I don't see her anywhere, I get a sinking feeling in the pit of my stomach.

I check the women's restroom to find it empty. A quick survey of the employee lounge shows it empty too.

I head to Tony's office and walk in without announcing myself.

Tony looks up with a scowl until he sees it's me, and then his face smooths over before he frowns himself when he sees what is undoubtedly a harried, worried look on my face.

"Damon, how can I—"

I cut him off with, "Have you seen Hadley?"

"She left the floor about fifteen minutes ago. I haven't seen her since. I assumed she left a little early considering all that happened today, so I didn't say anything about it."

"Why? What's wrong?" Tony calls after me, but I'm already leaving his office.

I pace back and forth in the hallway like a lion, my thoughts going a hundred miles a minute.

Why would she just not show up? Did I hurt her when I took her so roughly on her break? She'd begged me to go harder. I thought she wanted it rough, but what if I went too hard? What if I scared her with my intensity and the filth I whispered in her ear?

I remember how her pussy clenched around me, though, and know that's not it. My perfect little angel loves it when I talk filthy to her when I'm inside her—whether she'd ever admit to it or not.

My next train of thought is that piece of shit stepdad of hers, but I know he hasn't been back to the restaurant because I've kept a careful eye on the place after I left. Not only had I been obsessively checking myself in between servicing cars, but I had Tony watching too. He was here nonstop. Surely he'd have noticed if the fucker came back in.

So what the fuck is it? What's going on? Where is Hadley?

I walk back into the employee area and notice a slip of paper laying on the floor. I pick it up to throw it in the trash for Tony, but I pause when I see writing on it.

I read the message, and my vision goes red.

There's no name signed on the note, but it's obvious who wrote it and who the recipient was.

And it's also blatantly obvious to me where Hadley's gone and why. The fucker threatened me, and my precious girl was offering herself up like a sacrificial lamb to save me.

I pull my cell phone out and ring Hadley, and I hear the ring coming from one of the employee lockers.

"Goddammit!" I curse. She left her cell phone behind so she couldn't be reached or traced.

I dial another number on my phone. "What have you got for me?" I ask without introducing myself. Who I've called knows who I am. I had my guy do a complete profile on Randal fucking Stevens, and I needed to know his address now.

I wait as he begins rattling off criminal history before I interrupt him. "I need the address right now."

He stops mid-sentence before reading it off to me.

I commit it to memory and hang up the phone

before resolutely heading back out to my SUV, taking the information about who Randal owed and placing a few other phone calls on my way.

I'm coming Hadley.

Hadley

"Well, well, well," Randal gloats as I walk woodenly through the door to the home I never wanted to see again. "Look what the cat dragged in."

I don't say anything. There's no sense in arguing with Randal. He's got me now. He has leverage, and he knows it.

"Come here, babygirl, so I can welcome you home properly." His words are a bit slurred, and it's obvious he's already been drinking.

My eyes flick over to my mother who's passed out asleep on the couch. Oblivious to everything going on —again.

Randal's eyes follow my line of sight. "Don't worry about her. She'll be out for the rest of the night. It's just you and me, babygirl."

"Come here," he says again.

Still, I don't move. I can't. I'm glued to the spot.

His eyes narrow at me. "I said come here, Hadley. Don't make me say it again."

I feel the dread settle in my stomach as I force my feet to move over to where he's standing with his arms outstretched.

I can't bring myself to step into his embrace, but it turns out I don't have to because he takes the last couple of steps and pulls me into him.

I feel his belly between us, but he presses his hips into me, and I feel the bulge of his erection press against me too. I feel the bile starting to rise in my throat, and I instinctively pull away from him.

God, I don't know if I'm strong enough to endure this. I know what he wants.

"You be a good girl and nothing will happen to that felon you like so much," he reminds me.

I close my eyes and try to focus on not breathing in the rank smell of his alcohol-laced breath.

"Did you let him pop your little cherry?" Randal asks me. "Hmm?" he prompts me when I don't answer.

He suddenly yanks hard on my ponytail, forcing me to look up at him. "Did you writhe and moan for him like a cock-hungry little slut?" He looks angry, but I feel him grow harder against me like the thought of it turns him on.

I stare up at him defiantly, glad that if I'm going to

be raped by this disgusting pig that at least Damon was my first. Randal will never be able to take that from me.

As if he can read my thoughts, Randal frowns down at me, "That little cherry should have been mine, you know. I've been taking care of you all these years, waiting for you to grow up, and then you go out and give it away to some fucking grease monkey."

I find it hilarious that Randal would have the nerve to trash Damon's profession considering that he himself hasn't held a job in years. He works one odd job after another, and when he does get fortunate enough to get something permanent, it never lasts more than a couple of weeks before he fucks it up.

"You're not even half the man he is," I tell him with all the contempt I can muster.

Randal's face turns red with anger as he sputters down at me. "I'll show you how much of a man I am, you little bitch." I feel his spittle rain down on my face, but I'm not sorry for what I said.

He raises back his hand to strike me, and I flinch before I ever feel the hit.

I hear a loud crack and wonder if he hit me so hard I can't feel it, but then I hear an animalistic roar that doesn't sound anything like Randal.

I open my eyes and look up to see Randal with his feet dangling out from underneath him.

Damon's got him held up by the collar of his shirt, and he pulls his fist back and slams it forward, connecting with Randal's face.

I hear the crunch of bone as Damon breaks his nose. Randal wails, his hands clutching his face where blood spurts from it.

Damon pulls back to swing again, but I stop him with a cry of his name, "Damon!"

I don't give a shit about Randal and could care less if Damon beats him to a bloody pulp. It's what he deserves, but I'm thinking of what would happen to Damon if he kills him. I don't want him to go back to prison, away from me.

Damon pauses, looking over at me, his eyes wild.

"He's not worth it," I tell him gently.

"He fucking touched you!" Damon bellows.

"I'm okay," I seek to reassure him. "You got here before he could do anything."

Damon looks back at Randal, a battle obviously raging in his mind. He wants to kill him, but he recognizes the wisdom in my words. Damon knows better than most the consequences of being locked up.

He drops Randal with a rough shake, and Randal falls to the floor in a heap, still groaning over his nose.

Damon comes to me and wraps his arms around me, and I collapse against him. His touch is my undoing, and the sobs suddenly come pouring out of me. "He said he was going to send you back to prison if I didn't come back," I sob against his chest, "and I couldn't let him do that."

"I know, sweetheart," Damon's stroking my hair soothingly. "But there's no way in hell anyone is taking me away from you. You should know that by now." He lifts my chin and gently reprimands me, "You should have come to me."

I sniff and nod, seeing that now. "How did you find me?" I ask him.

"I'll always find you," he tells me.

"You fucker!" Randal suddenly spits from where he's still crouched on the floor. "I'll have you locked up for this! I've got some friends in high places!"

Damon looks down at him with disgust before he says, "And I've got some in low places. Some who've been looking for you."

I don't really know what he's talking about, but Randal's face changes from anger to fear in a flash.

The next moment a couple of burly guys with wicked grins walk through the open door.

"Randal, my man," they say. "We've been looking

all over for you. You're a slippery little fucker. We'll give you that."

They nod to Damon, who simply nods back at them before he starts to usher me out of the door.

I glance over at my mom. She still hasn't stirred amidst all the commotion.

I don't know what the guys are planning on doing to Randal, but something tells me it's not good. I grab Damon's arm, and he looks down at me. "They won't hurt Mom, will they?" I ask him. I don't know why I'm so worried about her. It's not like she gave a shit about me all these years that she stuck me with Randal.

"No one hurts the woman," Damon tells them.

I watch them glance over to her and see she's passed out cold anyway.

"Done," they immediately agree.

"Come on, sweetheart," Damon tells me.

He leads me out of the house and to his car, but before he opens the passenger side door to let me in, he presses me up against it, staring down into my eyes intensely.

His gray eyes are stormy as he holds my gaze. "Don't you ever run from me again," he tells me, his voice breaking. "I don't give a fuck what the reason is. You come to me with anything. Anything. You hear me?"

He grips my face in between his huge hands, and before I can answer, his lips descend upon mine. His tongue thrusts into my mouth, claiming it insistently. I can feel his hands shaking where they hold my face, and I move my own to cover his, humbled by the emotion pouring out of him for me—*me*.

"You're mine, Hadley," he growls possessively when he finally pulls back from me.

"Yes," I tell him. "Yours. Always."

With another growl, he kisses me again.

Five Years Later

Hadley

I PLACE the phone back in the cradle after I book the last appointment before we close. I stand and look out of the office window into the attached garage where my husband works under the hood of a black Mustang.

I watch the muscles in his back ripple with every movement he makes and instantly feel moisture gathering between my thighs.

He looks up as he closes the hood, and his eyes meet mine.

After all these years, the intensity in his gray eyes hasn't faded a bit. If anything, he somehow manages to look at me even more intensely now.

He walks over to the sink in the corner of the garage and makes short work of washing his hands and forearms that are covered with grease from working on engines all day.

Damon is a hard worker, and that's just one of the many things I love about him.

He started up his own garage just a couple of years ago, and of course, he asked me to give up my job as a waitress to manage the office. He said he'd feel better having me close where he can make sure I'm okay at all times. Of course, we don't have to worry about my stepdad anymore. I'm not entirely sure what happened to him that day, but I haven't seen or heard from him since then. I think Damon knows what became of him, but I don't ask because I don't really care. I trust Damon when he tells me that Randal will never bother me again.

I'm not sure what became of my mom. I'd like to say that she got sober and that she's now a part of my life, but that would be a lie. The last I heard, she hooked up with a new guy, though if he's anything like the kinds of guys she usually hooks up with, he's nothing but trouble. It saddens me to think of how my mom is, but I think I gave up on her a long time ago. Maybe she'll get her shit together one day, but if I'm being realistic, I know that she probably won't.

Anyway, I book the appointments and handle the financial side of the business while Damon and a few guys he hired handle the manual labor side of things.

The guys Damon hired are also felons who needed a second chance. Of course, he carefully vetted them and made sure he only hired ones who were sincerely looking to turn over a new leaf, ones who, like him, had gotten in over their head when they were younger.

I'm so proud of Damon. He's an amazing boss, an amazing husband, an amazing father. He's just an amazing man period.

I think of how gentle he is with our four-year-old daughter, Paige. She's the spitting image of me with dark hair and my small frame, but her gray eyes are all her father's. And they go stormy just like his do when she's upset about something. Of course, she thinks he hangs the moon. And it's no wonder the way he spoils her, buying her damn near everything she wants within his power to give her.

Of course, there's another reason Damon likes to have me working in the office. When he takes breaks, he can pull me into the back room and fuck me as much as he wants. That's why I always wear dresses or skirts to work now—to give him easy access and because I love the way his eyes roam to my legs when he's working. He doesn't go an hour without looking in the office at me, his eyes clouding over with a mixture of lust and love every time he does so.

I'm so lost in my thoughts I don't even notice when Damon comes into the office until I feel him wrap his arms around me, pulling my back against his chest.

"What are you thinking of, wife?" he asks me while pushing my hair aside to lay a kiss on my neck.

I lean my neck to the side to grant him better access to it, loving the feel of his lips on my skin. I usually wear my hair up in a ponytail when we're at work, but I've had to wear it down the past couple of days to hide the hickeys and bite marks he left there during one of our rougher love-making sessions.

I know a lot of women don't like the look of hickeys, but I get a shiver every time I look at them, remembering how thoroughly Damon claimed me.

I see his reflection in the glass as he runs a finger over the marks he made, the look on his face proud. Damon loves leaving marks on me, a visible sign of his claim on me.

"I was thinking of how amazing my husband is," I tell him honestly.

"Oh?" he says, a cocky smirk on his face. "Is he the one who gave you these marks?" he asks me.

"Um-hmm," I answer, pressing my ass back against his hardness.

He groans and rocks his hips against me. "He's one lucky bastard," he says, his breath fanning against the lobe of my ear before he kisses right behind my ear, sending heat spiraling throughout my core.

"Damon," I half moan, half plead, tipping my head back.

He knows exactly what I want and lowers his lips to mine, his hand wrapping around my throat possessively as he angles my head up and holds me in place for his tongue to plunder my mouth.

I whimper, melting against him, and he pulls the back of my dress up, running his hands along my ass.

"Goddamn, sweetheart," he murmurs against my lips as his fingers dip under my panties to find me soaking wet. "That pussy is weeping for my cock, isn't she?"

I just mewl in response, and Damon removes his fingers. I almost cry in protest, but he gently grasps my wrists and moves my palms to the glass, silently telling me to hold myself up. My back instinctively arches, and Damon hisses in a breath as my butt pops backward.

"Damn, baby, that's what I'm talking about," he says, and I hear the zip of his pants. My pussy gets even wetter in anticipation, knowing that it's about to be filled.

He pulls my panties to the side and rubs the head back and forth along my slit, gathering up the wetness there before he thrusts deep within me.

I'm so wet that he slides fully into me in one hard thrust, the tip of his cock hitting my cervix. I can't stop the cry that leaves me, and he moans deeply as my pussy clenches around him.

"Fuck, honey, that little pussy is already falling open on me, isn't it?" He punctuates his statement with another thrust, and I explode, coming faster than I ever have in my entire life.

"Oh, god, Damon," I whimper as he begins to pump up into me, his hands on my hips, riding me through my orgasm that seems to go on forever.

"Motherfucker," he groans out in between clenched teeth, "if your little pussy keeps sucking me off like that, I'm gonna get you pregnant again, sweetheart."

I cry out as another wave of pleasure washes over me, and then I feel Damon's breath hot against my ear.

"You like that, don't you, baby? You want me to nut all up in you and knock you up again, don't you?"

"Damon!" I scream.

"Oh, fuck," his breathing becomes more ragged as he pumps up into me harder and faster, the wet, filthy sounds of our sexes slapping together filling the room.

"Fuck, Hadley, I'm coming in you, baby," he tells me right before he lets out a soul-wrenching groan, clasping me tightly against him.

I feel the jets of his come spurting up into me, filling me with his heat until it begins to trickle down my thighs.

"I love you, Damon," I tell him, my voice shaky in the aftermath of our passion.

"I love you too, sweetheart," he tells me with a kiss to the back of my head, "so fucking much."

THE END

Connect with Emma!

Visit Emma's website to get a FREE book you can't get anywhere else: www.authoremmabray.com.